A NOTE TO PARENTS

Disney's First Readers Level 1 books were developed with the beginning reader in mind. They feature large, easy-to-read type, lots of repetition, and simple vocabulary.

One of the most important ways parents can help their child develop a love of reading is by providing an *environment* of reading. Every time you discuss a book, read aloud to your child, or your child observes you reading, you promote the development of early reading skills and habits. Here are some tips to help you use **Disney's First Readers Level 1** books with your child:

★ Tell the story about the original Disney film or video. Storytelling is crucial to language development. A young child needs a language *foundation* before reading skills can begin to emerge.

★ Talk about the illustrations in the book. Beginning readers need to use illustrations to gather clues about unknown words or to understand the story.

★ Read aloud to your child. When you read aloud, smoothly run your finger under the text. Do not stop at each word. Enliven the text for your child by using a different voice for each character. In other words, be an actor—and have fun!

★ "Read it again!" Children love hearing stories read again and again. When they begin reading on their own, repetition helps them feel successful. Maintain patience, be encouraging, and expect to read the same books over and over.

★ Play "question and answer." Use the After-Reading Fun activities provided at the end of each book to further enhance your child's learning process.

Remember that early-reading experiences that you share with your child can help him or her to become a confident and successful reader later on!

— Patricia Koppman
Past President
International Reading Association

Disney's THE LITTLE MERMAID
Ariel's Treasure Hunt

by Patricia Grossman
Illustrated by Sol Studios

Disney's First Readers — Level 1
A Story from Disney's *The Little Mermaid*

SCHOLASTIC INC.

New York Toronto London Auckland Sydney
Mexico City New Delhi Hong Kong Buenos Aires

In her secret sea cave,
Ariel finds an old,
old map.

"Will we find the treasure?" Sebastian asks.

Ariel and Sebastian swim out of the cave.

They follow the map.

They swim into
an old ship.

There is
no treasure
there!

They follow the map.
They swim up
to Scuttle.

They swim down
to the sea floor.
There is no
treasure there!

They follow the map.
They swim under
the reef.

They swim over
the sleeping shark.

They follow the map.

They swim in front
of the glowing ball.

They swim behind
Flotsam and Jetsam.
There is no
treasure there!

The map leads them
back to Ariel's cave.
They find Flounder there.
Ariel cries, "A friend
is the best treasure!"

AFTER-READING FUN

Enhance the reading experience with follow-up questions to help your child develop reading comprehension and increase his/her awareness of words.

Approach this with a sense of play. Make a game of having your child answer the questions. You do not need to ask all the questions at one time. Let these questions be fun discussions rather than a test. If your child doesn't have instant recall, encourage him/her to look back into the book to "research" the answers. You'll be modeling what good readers do and, at the same time, forging a sharing bond with your child.

1. Who follows the map with Ariel?

2. What do Ariel and Sebastian think they're going to find?

3. Where do Ariel and Sebastian finally find the treasure?

4. What kinds of treasures can you name?

5. What is a treasure?

6. Name some underwater things from the story.

Answers: 1. Sebastian. 2. a treasure. 3. in Ariel's cave. 4. possible answers: money, gold, silver, jewelry. 5. something very valuable. 6. possible answers: seaweed, seahorses, old ship, clam shell, starfish, rocks, sand, reef, shark.